The Golden Vanity

The Golden Vanity

By John Langstaff

With pictures by David Gentleman

HARCOURT BRACE JOVANOVICH, INC.
NEW YORK

This book is affectionately dedicated to Douglas Kennedy, from whom I first heard the ballad of *The Golden Vanity* when I was a young boy. He sang his family's variant to this tune:

Briskly

There was a gal - lant ship, and a gal - lant ship was she;

Eek! did - dle dee to the Low - lands low, and she was called the

Gold - en Van - i - ty, as she sailed to the Low - lands low.

ISBN 0-15-231500-4

Library of Congress Catalog Card Number: 76-167835

Printed in the United States of America

First edition

B C D E F G H I J

PREFACE

For more than three hundred years this sea story has been sung by people in England and Scotland. British sailors and early colonists must have brought it along with them to this country so that it became one of the first songs transplanted to the United States. It is a *ballad,* a traditional story that is sung, the way people sang the stories about Robin Hood to one another long before they were written down in books to be read. It's the kind of story you will never forget once you learn to *sing* it!

The earliest the ballad seems to have been noted down was about 1650. Samuel Pepys owned a copy of it. At that time it was thought to be a true story concerning the famous seaman Sir Walter Raleigh, whose ship, the *Sweet Trinity,* was attacked by an enemy galleon while sailing in the Lowlands and was rescued by the daring of his cabin boy.

> Sir Walter Raleigh has built a ship
> In the Netherlands,
> And it is called the Sweet Trinity
> And was taken by the False Gallaly
> Sailing in the Lowlands...

Of course, the story was fictitious, notwithstanding the fact that Raleigh did have a daughter and was reputed to be an arrogant, selfish captain.

As the ballad spread throughout the United States and parts of Canada, changes were made in the names of the two vessels, from the *Sweet Trinity* to the *Holy Trinity;* the *Gold China Tree;* the *Merry Golden Tree;* the *Gallant Victorie;* the *Golden Willow Tree;* the *Silver Familee.* The *False Gallaly* changed to the *French Gallolee;* the *Turkey Revelee;* the *Turkish Rosalie!*

Because so many people have sung this narrative tale for so long, there are many different versions of both the music and the words. For this book, I've chosen my favorites from the variants people have sung and still do sing today on both sides of the Atlantic Ocean.

JOHN LANGSTAFF

There was a gallant ship from the North Country,
And she was called the Golden Vanity
As she sailed on the Lowlands, Lowlands low,
As she sailed on the lonesome sea.

She had not sailed a league, a league but barely three,
When she was overtaken by the Turkish Robberie
As she sailed on the Lowlands, Lowlands low,
As she sailed on the lonesome sea.

Then out spoke the Captain, out spoke he,
"I fear we will be taken by the Turkish enemy
As we sail on the Lowlands, Lowlands low,
As we sail on the lonesome sea."

Then up spoke the cabin boy, up spoke he,
"What will you give me if I sink the enemy
As she sails on the Lowlands, Lowlands low,
As she sails on the lonesome sea?"

"Oh, I will give you gold, and I will give you store,
And you shall wed my daughter dear when we are back on shore
If you sink them in the Lowlands, Lowlands low,
If you sink them in the lonesome sea."

The boy took a brace and bit, and overboard jumped he,
And he swam till he came to the Turkish enemy
As she sailed on the Lowlands, Lowlands low,
As she sailed on the lonesome sea.

Then out of his pocket his auger he drew
And bored nine holes for to let the water through
As they sailed on the Lowlands, Lowlands low,
As they sailed on the lonesome sea.

Now some were playing cards, and some were throwing dice,
And some were sitting by, giving very good advice,
As they sailed on the Lowlands, Lowlands low,
As they sailed on the lonesome sea.

Then some they ran with coats, and some they ran with caps,
To see if they could stop the saltwater gaps
As she sank in the Lowlands, Lowlands low,
As she sank in the lonesome sea.

Then the boy swam back to his own ship's side,
Saying, "Captain, pick me up, for I am drifting with the tide,
For I'm sinking in the Lowlands, Lowlands low,
For I'm sinking in the lonesome sea."

"Oh, I'll not pick you up again," the Captain he replied,
"I will give you no reward, I will leave you in the tide
As we sail on the Lowlands, Lowlands low,
As we sail on the lonesome sea."

Then out cried the cabin boy, out cried he,
"Then I'll sink you in the same way as I sank your enemy
As you sail on the Lowlands, Lowlands low,
As you sail on the lonesome sea."

So they threw him o'er a rope, and he swam close to the side,
And his messmates pulled him up from the fast drifting tide
As they sailed on the Lowlands, Lowlands low,
As they sailed on the lonesome sea.

Then the Captain gave him gold, the Captain gave him store,
And the Captain rewarded him far better than his word
As they sailed on the Lowlands, Lowlands low,
As they sailed on the lonesome sea.